D0460980

KAUGJAGJUK

BY MARION LEWIS · ILLUSTRATED BY KIM SMITH

Published by Inhabit Media Inc.
www.inhabitmedia.com

Inhabit Media Inc. (Iqaluit), P.O. Box 11125, Iqaluit, Nunavut, X0A 1H0
(Toronto), 146A Orchard View Blvd., Toronto, Ontario, M4R 1C3

Design and layout copyright © 2011 Inhabit Media Inc.
Text copyright © 2011 by Marion Lewis
Illustrations copyright © 2011 by Kim Smith

Editors: Neil Christopher and Louise Flaherty
Author Mentor: Ibi Kaslik
Art Director: Danny Christopher

Library and Archives Canada Cataloguing in Publication

Lewis, Marion, 1975-
Kaugjakjuk / by Marion Lewis ; illustrated by Kim Smith.

ISBN 978-1-926569-39-0

1. Inuit--Juvenile fiction. 2. Inuit--Folklore.
I. Smith, Kim, 1986- II. Title.

PS8623.E9665K38 2011 jC813'.6 C2011-904126-X

Canada Council   Conseil des Arts
for the Arts   du Canada

We acknowledge the support of the Canada Council for the Arts for our
publishing program.

Printed by MCRL Overseas Printing Inc. in ShenZhen, China.
August 2011 #4236067-4

KAUGJAGJUK

by Marion Lewis • Illustrated by Kim Smith

INHABIT
MEDIA

Dedicated to my Father.

Foreword

In early, youthful days, I was fascinated by stories.

Listening to tales or fables passed on from our ancestors, I learned about the strange existence of giants and other creatures from the past.

But one of my favorite stories was about Kaugjagjuk, a boy who became a hero despite the fact that he was a neglected orphan. He was determined, and he made himself become a strong human being.

Through his perseverance and the strength of his will, Kaugjagjuk became a strong living legend.

Mark Kalluak

The two young children, brother and sister, sat huddled on a whale-sized chunk of ice. Their teeth chattered; their warm breath escaped from their young lungs in ribbons of mist. Though the terror was behind them, their small bodies were still tense with fear. The girl began to sob quietly into her brother's shoulder. She wept, and as the boy patted her back absently he tried to piece together the horrible happenings of the morning.

Earlier in the day, Kaugjagjuk had watched his parents pack their sled as usual, preparing for the spring seal hunt. The family had travelled to the floe edge, where the sea ice meets the open ocean. Kaugjagjuk recalled breathing in the clear salty air as the dogs playfully bit at his ankles. At that moment, in the cool light of morning, he had felt the warmth of his family's love. Their movements were familiar and comforting; their voices surrounded him like a warm, fur-lined glove. He did not know then that his whole life was about to change forever in a single terrible moment.

While his parents busied themselves on one side of the floe, cutting ice and tending to the hunt, Kaugjagjuk and his sister played on the far side, distracted by the glassy ice and the open sky around them. Their excited laughter could be heard by the gulls that swooped above their heads. All of a sudden, a loud crack echoed like a thousand gunshots! The noise snapped the children out of their play. *Splash! Crack!* The ice around them had given way and broken apart into jagged pieces. It was as if a giant had sliced the sea ice with an ulu. The split in the floe was so severe it separated Kaugjagjuk and his little sister from their parents.

Kaugjagjuk was too stunned to speak. He stood like a stone figurine, clutching his little sister at his side. The two children stared at the deep icy gash of water that separated them from their parents. For many moments, Kaugjagjuk was unsure of what to do or say. He opened his mouth to speak but no words came out. His lips formed an empty circle as he and his sister drifted helplessly from the shore.

Amid the sounds of the seagulls, the distant weeping of his mother could be heard:

"Taqqiq, the Man of the Moon, is watching over you and knows when to help you! Do whatever he tells you to do, Kaugjagjuk! Taqqiq is your friend!"

"*Panilaa! Nagligivagit!* Little daughter! I love you!" cried their mother to her trembling daughter.

After the shock wore off, Kaugjagjuk began to worry that their icy boat would melt. He worried that a large sea mammal might capsize their ice pan; he fretted about how they would manage to survive without their beloved parents whose cries now seemed as far away as the distant sun. After many hours of crying, worrying, and trembling in the cold dusk, the tide docked their pan of ice on a distant shore. They were on land, at last. Kaugjagjuk and his little sister had survived.

They survived their experience on the ice, but for Kaugjagjuk, spring and summer were filled with more worry and loss. He spent most of these seasons scavenging for food. Kaugjagjuk knew that winter would make it difficult to find nourishment. His sister had become weak. Her skin had turned as sallow and sickly as dirty snow and she no longer laughed or played the way she had in the days when their family had been together. Although Kaugjagjuk had tried to cajole her out of her sadness with small treats of bird's eggs and games, she would not be comforted.

Then, on one of Kaugjagjuk's many hunts for food, he became separated from his sister. As they wandered through the mossy tundra, she disappeared into the landscape. She chose to follow a path away from her brother and he could not find her.

His heart heavy with loss, Kaugjagjuk wandered until he came across a small village. At first, Kaugjagjuk was overjoyed. Perhaps the villagers would know of his sister's whereabouts! Perhaps they knew what had happened to his parents! But there was no news of his family. There were no words of welcome or kindness for Kaugjagjuk because the people of this village were very cruel and unkind. Instead of welcoming the lost orphan, they put him to work. Instead of being given a comfortable place to rest, he was left to sleep in the porch with the dogs. From his first day in the village to nearly his last, he always struggled like an animal for his survival, forced to complete the most detestable of chores.

In the village, Kaugjagjuk's life had become one humiliating event after another. For many months, Kaugjagjuk had stoically completed all of his awful duties, the worst of which was to empty the communal chamber pots in the community iglu. In addition to these horrible chores, Kaugjagjuk was not spoken to like the other small children and, because of this, Kaugjagjuk began to lose his words. He began to communicate using only instinct and body language, like the camp dogs. Kaugjagjuk began to forget that he was human and he forgot his mother's parting words. He could not remember that she had told him the Man of the Moon was watching over him and cared for him. Slowly, all memories of human affection and kindness, along with his mother's words, slipped from his memory like a seal gliding underwater.

Every night, as on the first night, the people in the village did not permit Kaugjagjuk to enjoy the warmth of their iglus. Instead, he was made to sleep in the cold porch with the dogs. The dogs became very fond of Kaugjagjuk, so much so that one allowed the boy to use his furry belly as a pillow, while another kept the boy's tired feet warm during the freezing winters. A third dog became a comforting fuzzy mattress, whose rhythmic breathing lulled Kaugjagjuk's exhausted mind and body to sleep.

Kaugjagjuk was not yet the size of a man, but his heart had grown to love and appreciate the loyalty the dogs showed him. Kaugjagjuk's four-legged family had done well in keeping his body warm and comfortable during this difficult time, and the boy was very grateful for their animal kindness, especially in the face of the villagers' taunting and mistreatment.

Several years passed, and as Kaugjagjuk changed into a young man, he began to grow weary from lack of food and excessive work. The young man's dreams became flooded with images of Taqqiq, the Man of the Moon, and it was in one of these dreams that Kaugjagjuk began to remember his mother's words about this great man. And so, in his dreams, Kaugjagjuk began to petition Taqqiq for help.

The Man of the Moon's job is to watch all who sleep under the moon's gaze. Indeed, the moon is not as bright as the burning sun, but Kaugjagjuk understood that although the moon does not emit its own light, it does keep careful watch by supplying a bright light during the coldest and darkest of winter nights.

The moon's lesser light is made brighter still by the cold, unfeeling snow. The Man of the Moon's job is to reflect light onto all deeds and to record both the good and bad deeds of all those who sleep under the moon's gaze. When Taqqiq finally came down to our world to help Kaugjagjuk, the villagers saw nothing, heard nothing, and slept heavily through his visits.

Slowly, the Man of the Moon and Kaugjagjuk began their friendship, at night, during the secret time of dreaming. Meanwhile, none of the villagers noticed that Kaugjagjuk was growing into a man. Only the Man of the Moon could see the boy's heavy tracks in the snow. Only Taqqiq threw moonlight on Kaugjagjuk, creating a bright, blank canvas to illuminate his path. The villagers, on the other hand, were so nearsighted that they did not notice that the small orphan was growing up. Nor did these villagers possess the foresight to remember that what is small will one day grow to become big and strong.

The villagers would come to regret their selfishness and the light of the moon would expose their cruelty. The Man of the Moon, a benevolent, strong, and wise observer, would give Kaugjagjuk something that he had not known for many years: hope.

One night, when the Man of the Moon had decided the young boy had suffered enough, he warned the frightened orphan:

"I will come down to Earth and whip you. The whip's bite will represent the hardships you have suffered and the difficult times to come. But, when I ask you, 'Do you feel the whip's sting?' you must answer, 'No, I am not sore.' You see, little man, life is full of difficulties and you must persevere and push through these difficulties."

Although Kaugjagjuk did not completely understand the reason for the whippings—and hoped that his suffering would be short-lived—he was an obedient boy and agreed to do as Taqqiq said.

During the following full moon, when the villagers were asleep, the Man of the Moon came down to earth. He walked through the village unseen, and even the ever-watchful dogs respected his wish for silence. When he finally approached the porch where Kaugjagjuk was sleeping, he whispered the boy's name. Afraid, Kaugjagjuk summoned his courage and crawled out into the night air and stood up in front of Taqqiq. Silently, the Man of the Moon turned and walked out of the village, and the orphan followed.

When they arrived at a place where the wind had blown the snow off of the ground, exposing the rocks, Taqqiq faced Kaugjagjuk.

"Turn over the rocks," said the great man, pointing to several large stones.

Without pause, Kaugjagjuk chose one of the smaller rocks and bent down, trying to lift it. The orphan strained, but the rock was frozen to the ground and would not move. He tried again, but this time he heard the sound of Taqqiq's whip whistling through the air, and then felt the sting as it bit deep into his back. Kaugjagjuk remembered the man's words and clenched his teeth in order to silence his whimpers. Again the whip came down and, once again, Kaugjagjuk used his ability to withstand hardship and remained silent. He put his energy into heaving and flipping the heavy rocks in front of him.

The Man of the Moon whipped Kaugjagjuk six times. After each strike, the Man of the Moon asked the boy:

"Do you feel sore? Do you ache?"

Although Kaugjagjuk's muscles burned and his eyes swelled with hot tears of pain, he responded the way the Man of the Moon had instructed him: "No, I am not sore. I feel no pain at all." When he said this, he diligently continued to lift and upturn the heavy stones around his feet. Kaugjagjuk focused on the task at hand, not the bite of the whip, and soon he noticed that even the heaviest stones moved easily.

As the Man of the Moon whipped Kaugjagjuk six more times, the boy wondered why his mother had told him that this man was his guardian. Why would his guardian inflict so much agony upon his flesh? But, just as he pondered this question, the pain ebbed away and was replaced by a sense of power and strength.

After several more lashings, Kaugjagjuk began to feel even less pain: he was numb. By the end of the last beating, his tears had dried; his calloused skin had grown thick and tough; and his muscles were supple and strong from all the rocks he had heaved and flipped over. By the end, Kaugjagjuk had transformed into a very large and strong man.

The Man of the Moon saw this strength and told Kaugjagjuk that he was ready.

Kaugjagjuk wondered out loud what adversity awaited him next, and the Man of the Moon answered:

"I will be sending three large bears to the village. You are ready now to face them. You are strong enough."

Indeed, Kaugjagjuk had endured his suffering as a boy with great patience and, because of this, the Man of the Moon had shown Kaugjagjuk that he already had everything he needed within himself to become a strong and capable man.

The villagers would soon come to see that they had been wrong. They would soon learn that great abilities are indeed born in little bodies.

As promised, the Man of the Moon called three great bears to the village. Although Kaugjagjuk was now a great man, the villagers, ignorant and unfeeling as they were, still did not see that the small boy they had spent so many years abusing was now transformed. In their haste, they called out for Kaugjagjuk to be sacrificed to the three bears, whose teeth were as sharp and long as harpoons. There was panic in the village. The men and women screamed and ran about, but Kaugjagjuk remained calm as he walked towards the beach to greet the huge polar bears that were causing such terror. The villagers stopped screaming and crying for a moment; they did not recognize the large man before them.

"Here I am! The little boy you wished to sacrifice!" Kaugjagjuk said.

He mesmerized the crowd further by wrestling the bears, killing all three creatures with the ease and grace of an experienced hunter. The villagers were stunned into silence as they watched Kaugjagjuk casually throw the bodies of the massive animals into an enormous pile, as though they were no larger than baby seals. After the last bear had wheezed its final breath, Kaugjagjuk finally faced the awestruck villagers lined up in front of him. He asked them:

"Do you remember when you made me empty your dirty pots? Do you recall when you made me sleep with the dogs? Have you forgotten how you threw bones at me to eat because I was smaller than you?"

Kaugjagjuk, the mistreated orphan, had spared their lives and fought the powerful bears bravely. The villagers felt ashamed and looked to the ground, unwilling to meet the great man's gaze. They felt guilty about how cruelly they had treated the young boy. But their regrets meant little to Kaugjagjuk, who turned and walked away from the villagers. The dogs, his best and only friends, followed Kaugjagjuk out of the village. The boy, now a man, would never be hurt or shamed again.

Epilogue

The people of the village, in their selfishness and cruelty, had overlooked the potential greatness of a small child who would one day grow into a brave and loyal man. They felt shame and regretted their actions. They would always feel the loss of this great man, whose parting left a giant hole in the village. The villagers would never recover from this loss, and they would never forgive themselves for their selfish actions toward one small orphan who only required a few acts of kindness to flourish and grow. Their cruel behaviour and their callous and cold-blooded treatment of the orphan haunted them. Kaugjagjuk, with the proper nurturing and care, would have grown into a good, strong man who would have protected and provided for the villagers for a long time to come. But it was too late for their regret: they had lost Kaugjagjuk to the world forever.

The legend of Kaugjagjuk is an example of patience, perseverance, and hard work through adversity. Kaugjagjuk's endurance reminds all who experience similar difficulties that they, too, are strong enough to endure. The story of Kaugjagjuk reminds us that all—even the smallest and most downtrodden of us—may overcome neglect and great difficulties.

Through encouraging Kaugjagjuk to become stronger and resilient, the Man of the Moon helped the boy understand that hardship can produce perseverance, character, and strength.

Author's Note

The story of the orphan Kaugjagjuk is a traditional tale told throughout the Arctic. Traditional stories are living things—they are told and retold through families and communities, and, through this telling, the stories change. Across the regions of Nunavut, the story of Kaugjagjuk exists in many variations. In some versions, the orphan grows into an Inugaruligasugjuit, one of the lesser giants of Inuit mythology. In some versions, the torments that the villagers force Kaugjagjuk to endure are unimaginably terrible; in others, there are a few villagers who take pity on the boy. In almost every version of the story, Kaugjagjuk seeks ultimate revenge against his tormenters through swift and brutal violence.

But, in the story of Kaugjagjuk, I see more than just a tale of revenge. This is a brave story—an inspirational story—that illustrates a child's ability to overcome great difficulty and very real challenges.

Stories adapt to their storytellers and, with this book, I wanted to depict Kaugjagjuk as a boy who chooses mercy and forgiveness over cruelty and vindictiveness. I wanted to show that someone could rise above hardship and mistreatment, rather than perpetuate the destructive cycle of abuse.

I wanted to show that meekness does not equal weakness.

After you read this book, you may come across other versions of this story that end differently, or that portray Kaugjagjuk another way. Those stories are not wrong; they are just other living variations on this ancient story. In all his variations, Kaugjagjuk teaches us that great strength can grow from terrible adversity. And that's the lesson I hope you take away from reading this book.

Marion Lewis

About the Author

Marion Lewis was born in Iqaluit, Nunavut. She has lived in communities throughout the Arctic including Qikitarjuaq; Watson Lake, Yukon; and Inuvik. Marion was introduced to the imaginative and beautiful world of Inuit traditional stories while studying at the Nunavut Teacher Education Program in Iqaluit. That introduction sparked Marion's love for storytelling and inspired her to write *Kaugjagjuk*, her first book.

About the Illustrator

Kim Smith lives in Calgary, Alberta. This is her first children's book. When not illustrating for children, Kim illustrates comics. Her illustrations have been featured in advertising as well as in two comic collections, *The Anthology Project* and *The Anthology Project, Volume Two*. She graduated from the Alberta College of Art and Design in 2008 with a Bachelor of Design specializing in character design.

Iqaluit · Toronto
www.inhabitmedia.com